# Reading Together

# TEN IN THE BED

# Read it together

This story of *Ten in the Bed* is a variation on the traditional nursery rhyme which is well known to many children.

It's a memorable counting rhyme which helps children to count down from ten to one – and back again.

The gentle, detailed illustrations offer lots to talk about together. They provide the humour and the surprise of an additional story in which the toys fall out of bed!

There were ten in the bed and the little one said, "Roll over, roll over!"

What's the mouse doing?

He's going to fall in the potty!

Boo hoo. I'm cold. All come back!

The strong rhythm, rhyme and repetitive language of the story encourage children to join in the reading.

"Roll over, Roll over!"

...and the little one said ...

You may find that children use the story when playing with some of their own toys.

Why are all your toys on the floor?

With books they know well children can have a go at reading to you. Their enjoyment of the story is more important than getting every word right.

I say, "Roll over, roll over." And they all fall out!

We hope you enjoy reading this book together.

For Brian and Daphne

First published 1988 by Walker Books Ltd
87 Vauxhall Walk, London SE11 5HJ

This edition published 1998

2 4 6 8 10 9 7 5 3 1

Printed in Great Britain

ISBN 0-7445-4891-8

# TEN IN THE
# BED

# Penny Dale

WALKER BOOKS
AND SUBSIDIARIES

LONDON • BOSTON • SYDNEY

There were ten in the bed and the little one said,
"Roll over, roll over!"

So they all rolled over and Hedgehog fell out ... BUMP!

There were nine in the bed and the little one said,
"Roll over, roll over!"

So they all rolled over and Zebra fell out ... OUCH!

There were eight in the bed and the little one said,
"Roll over, roll over!"

So they all rolled over and Ted fell out ... THUMP!

There were seven in the bed and the little one said,
"Roll over, roll over!"

So they all rolled over and Croc fell out ... THUD!

There were six in the bed and the little one said,
"Roll over, roll over!"

So they all rolled over and Rabbit fell out ... BONK!

There were five in the bed and the little one said,
"Roll over, roll over!"

So they all rolled over and mouse fell out ... DINK!

There were four in the bed and the little one said,
"Roll over, roll over!"

So they all rolled over and Nelly fell out … CRASH!

There were three in the bed and the little one said,
"Roll over, roll over!"

So they all rolled over and Bear fell out ... SLAM!

There were two in the bed and the little one said,
"Roll over, roll over!"

So they all rolled over and Sheep fell out … DONK!

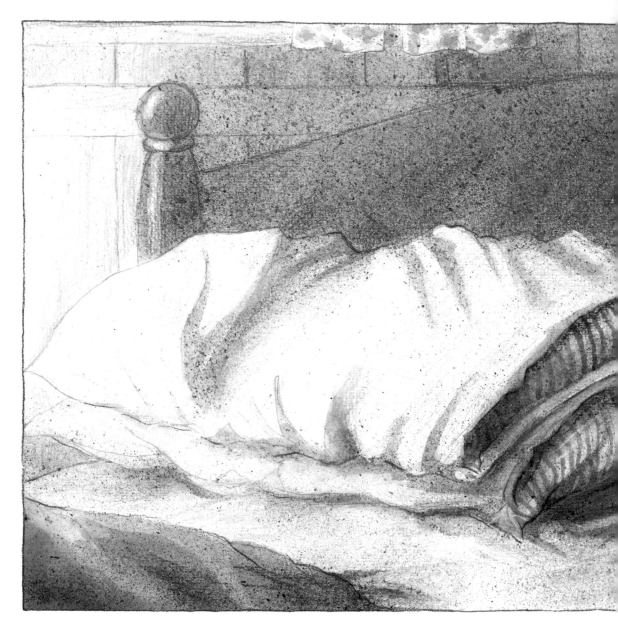

There was one in the bed and the little one said,

"I'm cold! I miss you!"

So they all came back ... and jumped into bed –
Hedgehog, Mouse, Nelly, Zebra, Ted,

the little one, Rabbit, Croc, Bear and Sheep.

Ten in the bed, all fast asleep.

# Read it again

### Joining in

As you read aloud, your child can
join in the story by saying the sounds
as each character falls out of bed.
At first these might all be "Bump!"
but as the book grows more familiar,
different sounds are likely
to be used.

So they all rolled ove
and Ted fell out ...

THUMP!

### Find the toys

You can use this picture to hunt through the book
to find and name each of the toys.

## Act it out

With some help, your child could collect together ten favourite toys. These can be placed in a line and used to act out the rhyme as you read it aloud.

## Tell the story

Talking through the pictures, encourage your child to tell the story of what the toys get up to when they fall out of bed.

Children can begin by describing the adventures of one toy, following the pictures through the book.

*Rabbit fell out!*

**Ted pulls the crocodile's tail and they all fall down.**

## Count it out

As you read the rhyme, you can look together at the numbers in the text, counting the numbers of toys *in* and *out* of the bed, for example 9 in and 1 out, 8 in and 2 out, 7 in and 3 out – making 10 in all.

A good way to do this is to use fingers, folding one finger down each time a toy falls out of bed.

**That's three in the bed.**

### Counting rhymes

There are many counting rhymes, some counting down like this one (10, 9, 8) and others counting up (1, 2, 3). You could look for others to share together like *Over In the Meadow; Five Little Ducks; Ten Green Bottles; One, Two, Three, Four, Five; One, Two, Buckle My Shoe* and different versions of *Ten In the Bed* too.

# Reading Together

The *Reading Together* series is divided into four levels – starting with red, then on to yellow, blue and finally green. The six books in each level offer children varied experiences of reading. There are stories, poems, rhymes and songs, traditional tales and information books to choose from.

Accompanying the series is a Parents' Handbook, which looks at all the different ways children learn to read and explains how *your* help can really make a difference!